Pearl 🐚 Diver

Book Three

UNDER THE SEA

Written by
ELLEN LEWIS

Illustrations by
MAX STASIUK

Pioneer Valley Educational Press, Inc.

CHAPTER 1

The Dive

Yousuf stepped closer to the edge of the pearling boat.

"Now!" cried the **Nakhuda** (*na-KOO-da*). "Go now!"

Yousuf's feet crashed into the water. It was warm. This wasn't a surprise. It was July, and the air temperature in the Arabian Gulf was 115 degrees.

He slipped through the waves and began to sink quickly — 25 feet, then 50. He looked around. His eyes blinked to get used to being open underwater. It was quiet. "It is almost as quiet and peaceful as the desert," he thought.

Like most **Bedouins** (*BED-wins*), Yousuf grew up in the desert. He had never been in the water until a few weeks ago. He was here now because his sister, Dalida, had gotten sick, and his family needed money to pay the medical bill. They had talked about selling their camel, but a Bedouin family without a camel was like a boat without a sail. They needed their camel to move from place to place in the desert. They would have a difficult time surviving without their camel.

When Yousuf decided to help his family by diving for pearls, his mother was afraid. She said that many divers never came up from the bottom of the sea. Yousuf tried not to think about that now.

There were four other divers nearby. Yousuf glanced around as they sank down, down, down. They floated past dark and frightening shadows. Each shadow seemed like it could be a shark waiting for them.

Last week, Yousuf had seen sharks in the water. The sharks' gray fins looked like knives cutting through the sea. Yousuf warned everyone of the sharks, and the men on the **dhow** (*dow*) played their drums to scare them away.

But Yousuf did not have a drum with him now.
If a shark saw him, he wouldn't be able to scare
it away like that.

Yousuf and the other divers sank deeper toward the reef where the oysters grew. Only a few of the oysters would have pearls inside. Once in a while, a diver would risk his life for a cluster of oysters, and there would not even be one pearl inside them.

Yousuf was sure that he would have good luck today. His family was counting on him.

CHAPTER 2
The Bottom of the Sea

Little clouds of sand drifted along the sea floor. Yousuf watched a school of tiny, bright orange-striped fish swim past him. He felt peaceful and calm.

The sea floor was covered with oysters. You
would have to be careful when he collected
The oyster shells were like very sharp knife bla
Some divers even wore little pieces of leather to
protect their fingertips as they grabbed and dug out
the oysters.

Yousuf swam closer to the reef. He quickly found a bed of oysters. He grabbed one of the oysters and pulled it away from the reef. Success! Yousuf grabbed the oyster before it sank. Then he shoved it into the basket that hung around his neck. He jabbed at the cluster to get the second one. It did not move. He pushed harder. Finally, it gave way. He stuffed it into his basket.

It took Yousuf almost a minute to collect six oysters. He began to feel a tight push in his chest. It felt like heavy rocks were sitting on him. He guessed that he had 45 seconds of breath left in his lungs. Then he would tug on the rope, and the **rope tenders** would pull him safely up to the surface.

Yousuf looked around for another bed of oysters. One of the other divers farther down the reef waved his arms. "What's wrong?" thought Yousuf. Then he saw dark shadows pass overhead.

Sharks. Just yards away from them were five, maybe six sharks. Huge, gray, frightening sharks. Yousuf tightened his hand around his lifeline, but he did not see the other divers pulling on theirs. "There must be a reason why they aren't signaling for help," he thought. "Maybe the sharks would grab them on the way up."

The sharks waved their massive bodies
from side to side in the water. Each one was as large
as two or three divers. Yousuf's heart pounded.
He would not stand a chance if they were hungry.

"*If* they are hungry?" Yousuf thought. "Of course
they are hungry. And we are a perfect meal for them."

CHAPTER 3

The Solution

"What should I do?" Yousuf thought.

Whenever he faced challenges back home in the desert, Grandfather would say, "Face your problems head-on. Don't run away!"

He had faced many problems head-on. That was part of everyday life for Bedouins. He had learned to stay safe in **shamals** (*sha-MALS*), sandstorms fierce enough to destroy a whole village. He had learned to find water in the middle of the desert. But how would a Bedouin know what to do in the ocean, surrounded by sharks?

The divers were trapped. And Yousuf was running out of air. He had to think fast.

Yousuf thought about how sad his family would be
if anything happened to him. He missed his family,
and he missed his old camel, Malloof. As a child,
Grandfather had taught him to care for Malloof.
Sometimes Malloof would become upset
about something and would spit at Yousuf.
Yousuf learned to look directly in the camel's eyes
and gently rub his nose until he calmed down.

One of the sharks approached Yousuf. He knew he had to do something. He quickly turned around to face the shark and held out his right hand.

The shark came closer. Yousuf looked into its wild gray eyes. Then he gently touched the shark's nose. The other divers watched in horror.

The shark shook its head from side to side. It looked at Yousuf. Then, to the amazement of the other divers, the shark relaxed. Yousuf carefully stroked the shark's nose, the same way he used to stroke Malloof's nose. The shark became calm and almost limp. After a moment, the other sharks swam away.

The other divers pulled on their ropes and began to rise through the water. Yousuf slowly pulled his hand away from the shark and tugged on his rope. The air rushed out of his lungs as he was jerked up.

CHAPTER 4

The Six Oysters

Yousuf struggled to breathe on the floor of the dhow. He did not know how he got there. He remembered being underwater, and now he was choking and gasping under the bright sun.

Yousuf's rope tender, the old man, turned him on his side. He slapped Yousuf's back a few times. Yousuf coughed the water out of his lungs.

Then Yousuf heard the other divers shouting.
"The Bedouin boy saved us!" they said.

"What happened?" asked the Nakhuda.

"A shark came at him, and he made it go to sleep.
  It was unbelievable! The shark just went still,
  and the other sharks swam away."

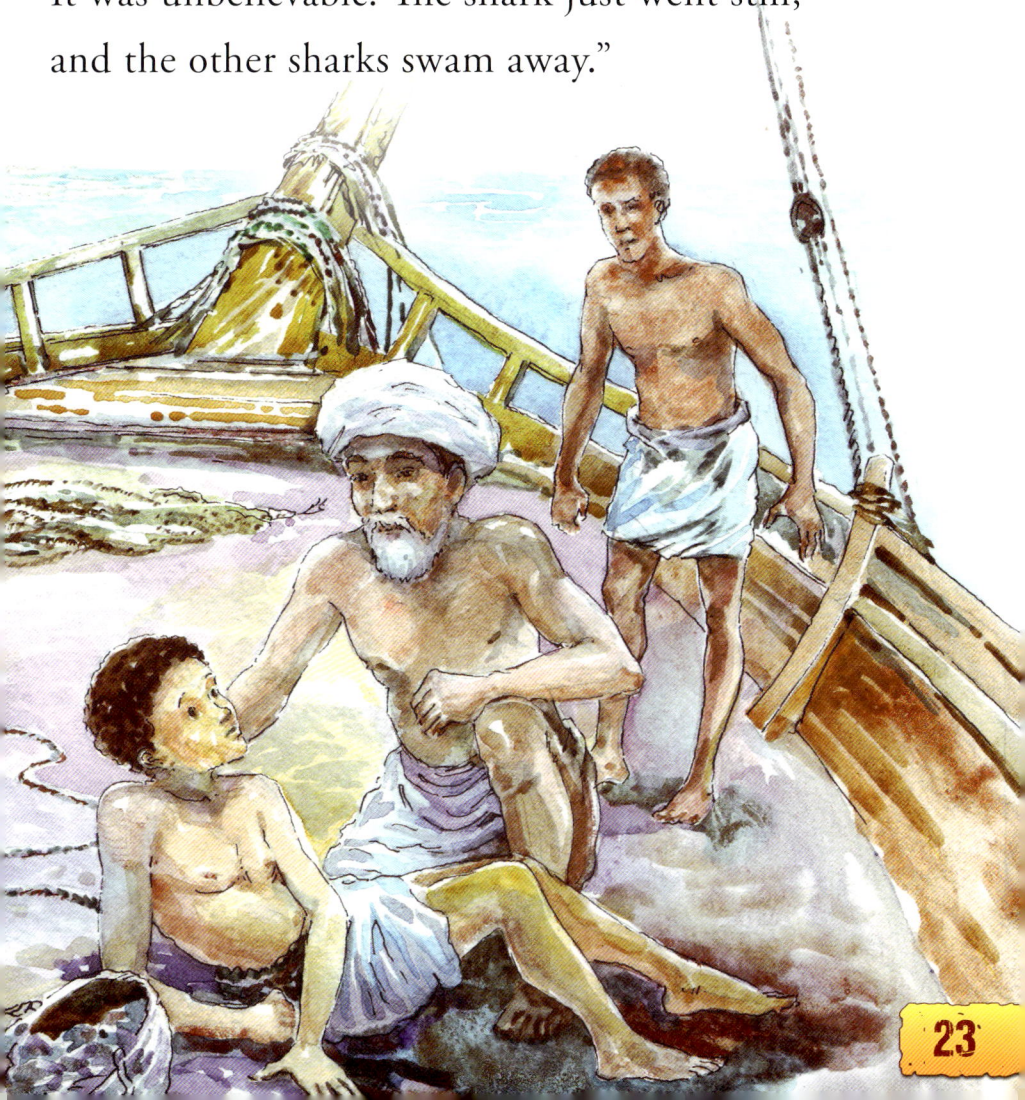

Yousuf sat up, exhausted. He could hear the others talking about him. He looked up at the Nakhuda.

The Nakhuda grunted. He gestured at the divers, and they all emptied their baskets onto the pile of oysters on the deck. Yousuf carefully placed his six oysters on top of the pile.

The Nakhuda walked toward Yousuf. Yousuf drew back. He knew he hadn't caught as many oysters as some of the other divers. He was afraid that the Nakhuda would yell at him.

The Nakhuda pointed at Yousuf's oysters. "Take them back," he said.

"I don't understand," Yousuf said. He was confused. Had he done something wrong?

The Nakhuda took Yousuf's oysters from the pile and held them out to him. "You saved the lives of our men today," he said. "We thank you by giving you these. Whatever you find inside them, you may keep for yourself."

The other divers gasped when they heard this.

"Thank you," said Yousuf. "You are very kind." He took the oysters from the Nakhuda.

"Now," said the Nakhuda. "Put those away and drink some coffee. We dive again in five minutes."

Yousuf nodded. He took the rest of his oysters from the pile and put them back in his basket. He would have to think of a safe place for them.

He thought of Grandfather. Somewhere in the middle of the desert, Grandfather had heard his cry from 50 feet under the sea.

The other divers brought Yousuf some sweet dates and coffee. They would be back in the water again soon, once the Nakhuda found another reef. But for now Yousuf was happy to sit and rest and tell the story of how Grandfather had helped him escape the sharks.